Police
Hurrying! Helping! Saving!

by **Patricia Hubbell**
illustrated by **Viviana Garofoli**

Marshall Cavendish Children

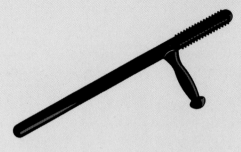

Marshall Cavendish Corporation
99 White Plains Road
Tarrytown, NY 10591
www.marshallcavendish.us/kids

Library of Congress Cataloging-in-Publication Data
Hubbell, Patricia.
Police : hurrying! helping! saving! / by Patricia Hubbell ; illustrated
by Viviana Garofoli. — 1st edition.
p. cm.
Summary: Illustrations and rhyming text celebrate police officers
and what they do.
ISBN 978-0-7614-5421-2
1. Police—Juvenile fiction. [1. Police—Fiction. 2. Stories in rhyme.]
I. Garofoli, Viviana, ill. II. Title.
PZ8.3.H848Pnp 2007
[E]—dc22
2007030156

The illustrations are rendered in digital art.
Book design by Vera Soki
Editor: Margery Cuyler

Printed in Malaysia
First edition
1 3 5 6 4 2

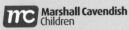

To retired Connecticut state police sergeant Martin A. Ohradan
—P.H.

To Emma and Abril
—V.G.

Thanks to Lieutenant David J. Dudeck, Jr.,
Princeton Borough Police Department,
Princeton, New Jersey, for his input.

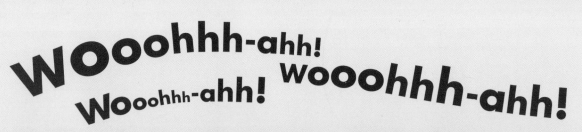

Wooohhh-ahh!
Wooohhh-ahh! wooohhh-ahh!

Police rush off to start their day.
Who knows what jobs will come their way!

The chief is head of the whole crew.

He checks on what the others do.

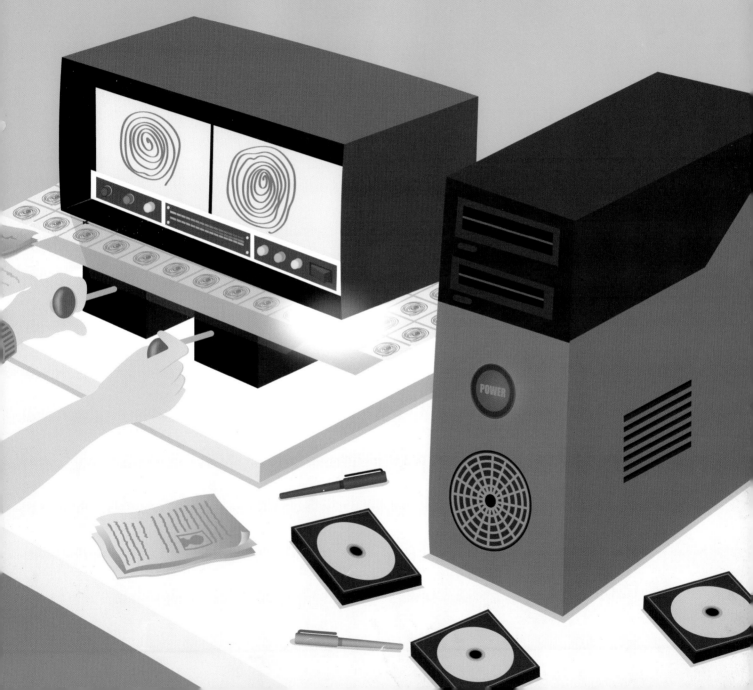

Solving crimes both old and new,
detectives look for every clue.

A patrolman walking on his beat chases a burglar up a street.

Police have dogs that search and find.

German shepherds. Steady. Kind.

Sometimes police bring dogs to school.
Dogs must obey! That is the rule!

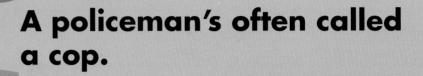

A policeman's often called a cop.

Some cops ride horses—

clip- clip- clop.

Police tell cars to stop! And go!
Tell speeding drivers to go slow.

They give directions. Give first aid.
They join parades. Lead motorcades.

Police help kids to cross a street.
Their gloved hands wave.
Their whistles tweet.

Police ride bikes.
They ride in cars.
Their shiny badges
glow like stars.

Police Department
9011-26

Sirens wail. **Wooohhh-ahh-wooohhh!**
Bright lights flash. Coming through!

Motorcycles swerve and vroom.

In boats that buck and zoom and roar, police patrol along the shore.

**When flames flare high
and smoke blows black,
police keep people safely back.**